Abigail
Iris

THE ONE
AND ONLY

Abigail Iris

THE ONE AND ONLY

Lisa Glatt and
Suzanne Greenberg

illustrated by Joy Allen

Walker & Company ✺ New York

First published in the United States of America in 2009 by Walker Publishing Company, Inc.,
a division of Bloomsbury Publishing, Inc.
Paperback edition published in February 2010
Visit Walker & Company's Web site at www.bloomsburykids.com

For information about permission to reproduce selections from this book, write to
Permissions, Walker & Company, 175 Fifth Avenue, New York, New York 10010

The Library of Congress has cataloged the hardcover edition as follows:
Glatt, Lisa.
Abigail Iris : the one and only / Lisa Glatt [and] Suzanne Greenberg ;
illustrated by Joy Allen.
p.   cm.
Summary: Abigail Iris thinks she would rather be an only child but after going on vacation
with her best friend, who is an "Only," she realizes there are benefits of being one of many.
ISBN-13: 978-0-8027-9782-7 • ISBN-10: 0-8027-9782-2 (hardcover)
[1. Brothers and sisters—Fiction. 2. Family life—California—Fiction. 3. Only child—
Fiction. 4. Best friends—Fiction. 5. Friendship—Fiction. 6. Vacations—Fiction.
7. California—Fiction.] I. Greenberg, Suzanne. II. Allen, Joy, ill. III. Title.
PZ7.G48143735Ab 2009   [Fic]—dc22   2008007391

ISBN-13: 978-0-8027-2071-9 • ISBN-10: 0-8027-2071-4 (paperback)

Book design by Yelena Safronova
Printed in the U.S.A. by Worldcolor Fairfield, Pennsylvania
2 4 6 8 10 9 7 5 3 1

All papers used by Walker & Company are natural, recyclable products
made from wood grown in well-managed forests. The manufacturing processes
conform to the environmental regulations of the country of origin.

To my nieces, Abigail and Sophia, each one a perfect vision. —L. G.

For my three One and Onlies—Joel, Noah, and Claire, whose insights into Abigail Iris earned her a pair of Heelys. —S. G.

To my grandkids—Rachel and Curtis (my San Fran buddies), Isaac, Mabel Joy, and little Luke. All are One and Onlies to me! —J. A.

Chapter 1

It's Saturday morning, and instead of watching cartoons, I'm following my mom around the house, pretending to help her clean. She pushes a dangling-over pillow back into the seat of the couch, and I push the same pillow in again, just to make sure it sticks this time.

"But everyone else has Heelys," I say.

There's a new hole in the side of my mouth where a tooth used to be. I put my tongue through it, but I make sure to keep my mouth closed so my mom doesn't think I'm sticking my tongue out at her.

"You know they are not in our budget, Abigail Iris," she tells me.

I follow my mom upstairs so we can put some more things back where they are supposed to go. She's a slower walker than I am, so I dance around a little on each step to avoid running into her on our way up.

Halfway to the top, she steps faster, and I stop dancing and we stomp the rest of the way up the stairs, our hands on our hips.

My mom turns around to look at me when we get to her bedroom, which is at the top of the stairs. I don't have time to move my hands.

"Abigail Iris," she says, and I think I might hear an earful about my rude behavior, but instead she sits down on the bed and pats the space next to her. "You know we can't spend money freely on everything you think you want. Do you know what being on a budget means?" she says.

"Yes," I say. "It means I am not the one and only child around here." *What it means*, I am thinking, *is no Heelys.*

"That's right," my mom says, "but you are the tickly-est." Then we are both on the bed,

silly and laughing, our fixing-up-things part of the day behind us.

൙

Here's what being on a budget means:

No Heelys.

No beach cruiser with handlebar tassels.

No cell phone.

No bedroom of my own to paint fairy-tale pink and enchanted purple.

I am in the third grade at Bayside Elementary School, and I have one sister and two half brothers and all of my three best friends are Onlies. The Onlies are the luckiest girls in all of the world, in my opinion, because they are not on a budget. The Onlies have Heelys and beach cruisers and get to go to ballet camp in the summer even though anyone can see that I am obviously a better dancer.

At Bayside Elementary, a person is not allowed to wear her Heelys. Even the Onlies have to skip or just plain walk across the playground to class like everyone else. Running is frowned upon. Skating is not allowed.

My three Only friends are named Cynthia, Rebecca, and Genevieve. I am best friends with each of them one at a time, depending on my mood. Cynthia is for my quiet moods, Rebecca is for my silly moods, and Genevieve is for when I've had it up to here.

There are two third-grade classes at Bayside Elementary, and two of my best friends are in the other class this year. Cynthia and Rebecca's teacher is the kind of person who likes to eat lunch by herself and take a little break, thank you, and she never lets her class out late even if they are terrible, unlike my teacher, Mrs. Aaronson.

Today I have had it up to here, so when Mrs. Aaronson finally lets our class out for lunch, a full three minutes after the lunch bell rings because some people cannot seem to line up properly in a nice straight line, I decide Genevieve will be my best friend today.

Instead of going right to lunch, though, I have to stop and tie my shoe in the hallway, and then I have to go all the way back to room 15 to get my lunch bag, which I nearly forgot in my desk. By the time I get to our regular spot at the picnic tables, Genevieve is already settled and has her napkin spread out in front of her like a place mat. She squints at me like she's been there for hours, waiting.

This is California, so we get to eat outside all year long unless it's raining. We hate, as a rule, to eat in the cafeteria. The cafeteria is loud and echoey and is full of the kind of rude people who will elbow your tray right off the table so they can squeeze in next to you even though they are not one of your three best friends.

"You are so lucky to be an Only," I tell Genevieve, sitting next to her and peering into my lunch bag to see if my mother stuck a last-minute surprise in there, like a package of cookies that she had hidden away. But all I see is my peanut butter and honey sandwich, my juice box, and my plastic bag of stick pretzels.

Genevieve takes her lunch out of her lunch box and lines it all up on her napkin place mat. She has California rolls, bottled water, raspberries, and a brownie.

"What's the problem this time, Abigail Iris?" she says, and sniffs at each of her six California rolls, making two rows out of them.

"My mom will not be convinced even though it is so obvious how much I need Heelys," I tell her, trading her a pretzel stick for a raspberry without asking. "I wish we could spend our money more freely, but we're on a budget."

"You need to make your case!" she practically yells at me. Genevieve's mother and father are both lawyers, and she is always telling everyone to make their case.

Cynthia and Rebecca sit down with their cafeteria trays across from us. This was definitely not a buying day, but they never read the menu like I do and just end up buying whenever they forget their lunches.

"Pork dippers," Genevieve says. "We should make a petition and get those things off the menu."

"I like them," Rebecca says, and then she dips one right into her applesauce and puts the whole thing in her mouth.

"I wish I remembered my lunch," Cynthia says, and I feel so sorry for her that I give her half my peanut butter and honey sandwich even though I had already decided that Genevieve is my best friend today.

"Billy is staring at the back of someone's head," Rebecca says to me, and holds her laugh in so hard, I can hear the air coming out of her nose.

"Give me a break. He's not staring at Abigail Iris's head," Genevieve says, but anyone can see by the way she turns around and sneaks a look that she's not 100 percent uninterested.

I, on the other hand, am truly not interested and decide to swipe another one of Genevieve's raspberries while she's not looking.

"Thanks for the sandwich," Cynthia says, chewing quietly.

After lunch, Cynthia and Rebecca skip rope together, and Genevieve and I pretend we don't care that they haven't bothered to include us. We walk around the playground, deciding what we are not too old to join in on. We pass the four square and the tetherball

and the reading girls sitting on the bench where you wait for your mom if she's late or, if you're Genevieve, for your nanny to pick you up. We end up at the swings and sit next to each other, half swinging, half just sitting because a person in third grade is too old for full-out swinging.

"Do you know what I've just now decided, Abigail Iris?" Genevieve says to me. "You're my true best friend, and you are the one that I'm inviting on spring break vacation."

"Really?" I say, and I almost stop swinging entirely.

"Yes, you're the one I'm picking to take."

I feel the sun on my back burning right through my shirt, the way it does when a person is on the blacktop too long, but I don't care. I keep sitting on that swing, my legs pumping now, even though I am nearing the end of third grade, not kindergarten, imagining my vacation with my Only best friend until the bell rings.

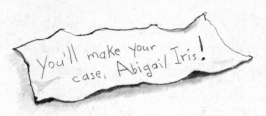

You'll make your case, Abigail Iris!

Chapter 2

After our spelling quiz, which I aced, I'm sure, since spelling is my best subject, I pass a note to Genevieve that says, *What if my mom and dad say no?* in my nicest cursive. Mrs. Aaronson is sitting at her desk with her glasses on, grading the quizzes, and we kids are supposed to be reading. I have my book in front of me and am pretending to read, but really I am waiting for Genevieve to hurry and pass me a note back.

Billy Doil, the boy who sits next to me, is in the bathroom, so I have to roll the note into a little ball and toss it at Shana, the girl who sits at the desk nearest Genevieve's. I'm waiting, looking down at my book like a good student, when Genevieve's responding note, also in a little ball, comes flying my way and lands by my tennis shoe, which *isn't* a Heely, by the way. I look around the classroom at the other students to make sure they're busy reading and then up at Mrs. Aaronson, who's still focused on our quizzes. I fake-cough into my hand and make sure no one cares that I might be getting sick before I lean down and snatch the note, all sly, because I don't want to get caught and be a disappointment.

Genevieve's note says, *You'll make your case, Abigail Iris.*

Mrs. Aaronson *does* look up then and gives me a small smile, which at first makes me suspicious, but then the smile grows and makes me think that she just graded my quiz and is pleased with my fine spelling ability. I give her a smile back and drop my hand on top of Genevieve's note to cover it up, even though Mrs. Aaronson obviously likes me a lot today and probably doesn't suspect a thing. I feel a little bit guilty for not paying attention to my book and decide to do just that right after I send my best friend one last note.

When Mrs. Aaronson goes back to her grading, I quickly write, *I'll make my best case.*

Billy Doil comes back to his desk then and he's huffing and puffing like he's had it with school and can barely stand one more minute here. He has what looks like dried ketchup on his chin, and I decide that he must have had the pork dippers for lunch. I want to motion for him to wipe his chin but more than that I want him to pass my note to Shana, so that she can pass it to Genevieve, and I don't want to make him mad by calling attention to his dirty chin, so I just smile and point at Shana and hand him the folded up note. Billy Doil always likes to be a part of everything so I should have guessed he'd read the note. But I didn't. He unfolds the paper and I can't help myself, the *No* comes out of my mouth before I have time to stop it.

Mrs. Aaronson looks up then and says, "What's going on over there, Abigail Iris?"

I open my mouth but nothing comes out, not my best case and not my worst case.

"Is everything okay, Abigail Iris?" she says, pushing her glasses up in the middle.

And I know she knows it's not okay, because she said both my names twice in a row, when usually she calls me just Abigail or even Abby, which I don't prefer, but don't ever say anything because she's the teacher with the grade book. Furthermore, she's pretty and nice.

Everyone looks at me, except Genevieve, who's biting her fingernail and pretending to be very interested in the book in front of her.

"I like to read," I say then, and lower my head and begin to do so.

❧

After school I wait with Genevieve, Cynthia, and Rebecca out front for our rides home. Billy Doil comes up and asks to talk to me, but I shake my head no and all my friends make a half circle around me. "Come on, Abigail, please," he says. My mother always reminds me to be polite, so that's all it takes— one "please" and a sad face, and I'm stepping out of the circle and letting Billy talk.

We're standing by the big oak tree and my friends are watching us and talking behind their cupped hands. Rebecca's making a funny face at me and Genevieve is shaking her head, all serious.

"Look," Billy says. "I'm not a good apologizer, but I feel real bad."

"You almost got me in trouble with Mrs. Aaronson."

Billy's looking at the dirt and moving one foot around in a circle. I try not to look at his nervous foot because it could make me dizzy. "I was hoping," he says. And then he stops. His cheeks are sort of pink and he's still got ketchup on his chin. It's more than dry. It's flaky now.

"What?" I say, sort of impatient.

"I mean, I thought the note was for me."

I shake my head like my mother does when I do something bad and then I see Billy's foot still moving and his face going pinker and I feel sad for him, so I wipe away the angry face. "It's okay," I say. "She didn't see."

We don't say anything for a minute or two, until I finally say, "Billy, you've got something on your chin. Right here," I say, motioning on my own chin.

Billy wipes his face with the back of his hand, then he looks at his hand and sees the ketchup. "Gross," he says.

"The important thing of the day is that Mrs. Aaronson didn't catch me. The rest of it doesn't matter," I tell him.

He looks up then, holds his foot still, and says, "Abigail Iris, you're a vision." And then he runs away.

A vision of what? I'm thinking. I walk back over to my friends and ask them, "Just what was Billy Doil talking about? A vision *of what?*"

"He probably heard that stuff in a movie," Cynthia says.

"I guess, but what's it mean?" I say.

They all shrug, and then I look for Eddie's car.

Eddie's my half brother. He is in high school, has seventh period free, and is coming to pick me up today. Because I'm getting a ride home with a teenager, I feel like the lucky one when usually my friends are the lucky ones because they are Onlies and have shinier cars or even a driver who isn't a mom or a half brother. Eddie lives with us only half the month, and he's always happy the first time each month he has to pick me up and show off the car he bought for $950 with his camp counselor–summer job money. Now, he pulls up with loud music on the radio, sort of dancing behind the wheel, smiling. My friends immediately start to giggle. Genevieve and Cynthia step back, but silly Rebecca moves close to the car and bends down to wave. "Hi, Eddie," she says, all bright and cheery.

"Hey there," he says to all of us.

When I get into the backseat, he makes the music quiet and turns around to look at me. "Do you want to ask your friends if they want a ride home?"

I shake my head. "Their moms are coming. And Genevieve's driver," I tell him.

"Whoa! Driver, huh? Fancy stuff, Abigail," he says.

Genevieve rushes up to the window then and whispers in my ear. "Make your best case," she says. I nod at her, all excited. She steps back from the car and the three of them are standing in a row now, waving 'bye. I wave too and so does Eddie before he turns his head around to make sure it's safe to go. Rebecca's jumping up and down and still waving when Eddie pulls into the street.

When we stop at a red light, I lean forward and correct him. "It's Abigail *Iris*. Don't forget the Iris part," I say.

"That's right," he says. "Sorry, baby sister."

"I'm *not* a baby," I say, trying not to whine.

"*Sorry* again," he says.

"It's okay," I say. And I can't help smiling because Eddie's smiling, and his smile is infecting.

"Tell me about your day, Abigail Iris," he says.

So I tell him about Genevieve and going on vacation and being worried about asking our parents and the first note I wrote and passed successfully and then the second note that Billy Doil intercepted and tried to read before I shouted out "No!" I tell him about almost getting caught and then I tell him about Billy Doil having ketchup on his face for over two hours and about him sort of saying he was sorry and calling me a vision.

"A vision of what?" he says. Except he sort of mumbles this instead of saying it directly because he has four fingers from the hand that's not on the wheel in his mouth. He looks like he's biting his nails, but he's only cleaning under them with his bottom teeth. This is the gross thing he started doing since he quit the habit of biting his nails so girls would talk to him.

"Exactly what I'd like to know," I say.

"I remember passing notes," he says, like he's sixty and not sixteen and hasn't passed a note in a million years.

"Do you think they'll let me go?" I say.

"Where?"

"On vacation with Genevieve."

"I don't know. They're pretty uptight these days," he says, putting both hands on the wheel as we get closer to the house. This is what he always says about our parents.

"I'm going to make my best case," I say.

"You're going to make *what?*" he says.

"Never mind," I say.

"Tell me," he says.

"Just turn up the music," I tell him.

Chapter 3

Later that afternoon, I'm upstairs in Eddie and Cameron's bedroom, jumping up and down with a paper thermometer in my mouth, helping Eddie with his science fair project and trying to plan my case in my head at the same time when I hear my parents come home from work.

"The teachers have arrived!" my dad shouts, the way he always does.

Eddie looks at his stopwatch and takes the thermometer from my mouth. "Still 98.6 degrees," he says, looking at it, worried. "Normal."

I tell Eddie I'm sorry that I'm so normal and leave him to walk downstairs and give my dad the greeting he expects. From the fourth-from-the-bottom stair I jump into his arms so hard it knocks the backpack right off of him.

"How's my amazing, fantabulous, nearing-the-end-of-third-grader?" he says to me.

"How's Old Man Cheeto?" I ask. That's my nickname for him because he's a snacker.

I can hear my mom already in the kitchen, opening the refrigerator and flipping on burners and waiting for me to get in there to give her a who-do-you-love hug, so I don't wait for my dad's answer. They're both teachers at the same high school, and unless someone has had such a terrible day that that person had to stay after for a special parent-teacher conference, they come home at the same time.

"Abigail Iris," my mom says to me, stopping all of her busyness for a minute. She bends down and squishes my ears into the side of my head so she can stare straight into my eyes better. "Who did I miss?" she says. Then she gets right back to work, chopping at tomatoes.

I look around the kitchen and figure out

we're having make-your-own-taco night, in honor of Eddie and Cameron's first night of the month with us. I can hear Cameron in the den, in front of the television, where he's supposed to be doing his homework. My sister, Victoria, is upstairs in our bedroom with the door closed, getting all of her homework done before she changes out of her school clothes or comes down to say hello to anybody.

Victoria and Eddie get As and Cameron gets Bs and Cs. The jury is still out on me because I'm only in the third grade and we don't get letter grades yet.

Thinking about the jury, I remember about the lawyer part and how I am supposed to make my case about going on vacation with Genevieve. The whole good feeling of the end of the day, with my parents home no longer missing me, almost stops entirely. I think that maybe if Eddie took my temperature now it would finally be higher because I feel so worried they're going to say no that I probably made myself sick.

I set the table with paper plates so we won't have to bother ourselves with lots of dishes on Cameron and Eddie's first night of the month with us. But I don't do anything special the way I sometimes do, like sneaking the fork partway under the bottom of the plate so the whole thing looks like a big lollipop. I'm too busy planning.

We always go camping over spring break, but if I am truly lucky, instead of camping I might get to go on a *real* vacation with an Only and stay in a hotel and order spaghetti and cheesecake from room service.

After everyone is finally seated at the table, my sister looking mad because she didn't get to finish her homework before dinner and would rather get back to it than make her own taco, my mom and dad smile at everyone a little before we eat.

This is the grace-saying moment at Cynthia's house, when I fold my hands up and try to look like I know what I'm doing.

We are half Jewish and don't say anything

resembling grace unless we're stuck at my grand-mom Ada's in Costa Mesa on a Friday night.

"I'm so happy everyone is together again," my mom says during the too-quiet grace-saying moment, and then Cameron helps himself to such a big spoonful of refried beans that he cracks his taco shell right open.

Then my dad starts asking Eddie and Cameron all sorts of boring questions about what they've been up to for the last two weeks, even though we talk to them on the phone almost every night and they live only eight blocks away. They're his children from mar-riage number one, so he's the one who gets to ask most of the questions. Cameron's talking about his teammate's dad, who got really angry when the other team won.

I clear my throat and look around the table, obviously ready to tell them something important, but no one seems to care.

"He took his baseball cap off and stomped on it," Cameron says, laughing. "Like a little baby."

"What an example of good sportsman-ship," my mom says.

My dad shakes his head.

"Yeah, get a life," Eddie says.

And everyone at the table is laughing but me, because I've still got my announcement to make and no one seems to remember that only seconds ago I cleared my throat and looked at them, all dramatic.

The Onlies do not have to spend their din-ners listening to the scores of baseball games. I bet when an Only has an announcement, the mom and dad put down their forks and knives and lean in to listen. I bet a cleared throat and a dramatic face is enough.

I clear my throat again, louder this time. "I have an announcement to make," I say.

Even Victoria looks at me, so I know I really said this and didn't just think about saying it.

"Hold on a minute," my mom says. "Let Cameron finish his story."

I look at Cameron and do not like him right now. I have a picture of him visiting me in the hospital on the day I was born. I have known him forever. I love him, but I do not like him this minute.

"Well, last week we won, but apparently not by enough because Steve's dad stomped on his baseball cap again."

"He's got a real problem, that one," my dad says.

"He needs to get a life," Eddie says again. "Hey, Vic," he says, "pass me the sour cream."

Victoria hates sour cream, so she doesn't want to touch the container, I can tell. She makes a face and scoots it across the table using one finger.

My mom looks at me. "Okay, now, Abigail Iris."

"Finally," I say.

"What is it, honey?" she says.

"I have been issued an invitation," I say.

"Yes?" my dad says.

I am quiet for what feels like a long time, almost losing all my nerve.

"Tell them, Abigail Iris," Eddie says.

"Genevieve chose me to be the one to ask on her spring break vacation with her, and I really think you should say yes and let me go or I will be so sad I may never be happy again." I look at my mom the whole time I say this because I know she is the one who will really make the decision.

And then I look at my dad because he hates to see me sad. "Not ever again," I say to him.

"What a drama queen," Victoria says.

"What kind of vacation?" Cameron says.

"A real one," I practically shout.

"Where?" my dad asks.

"At a hotel, obviously," I say, feeling frustrated now. "With room service!"

"Lucky," Cameron says.

"Well, her mother will have to call us and give us just a few more details," my mother says, helping herself to the grated cheese. "And then we'll just have to see, Abigail Iris."

"Fine," I say, not knowing if I'd made my case but glad that at least that was over with and I could relax and enjoy my dessert if there was one to enjoy.

It turns out that dessert is just leftover vanilla ice cream but my dad makes a big deal out of serving it, with chocolate chip eyes and mouths.

After dessert, when it's time to wash the pots and pans, I decide to care about my homework all of a sudden and let someone else help my parents for once.

Victoria is in the sixth grade, and she got our parents to put an old-fashioned-looking phone in our bedroom. It has a dial instead of buttons, so a person feels as if she's really making a phone call. One of the only good things about sharing a room is that when Victoria's not in there, I get to lie on her trundle bed with my shoes still on and use it.

"I made my best case," I tell Genevieve when she answers.

"I knew you would, Abigail Iris," she says. "I already started to make you up a packing list."

"I mean your mom still has to call my mom," I say, "and give her a few more details."

I'm wanting a few more details myself all of a sudden, but I'm embarrassed that I didn't already ask, and it feels like it might be too late now. "For example," I say, "where exactly is this hotel?"

"In San Francisco, Abigail Iris!" Genevieve says.

As far as I know, I've only been to one San ever. San Diego. I am speechless.

"Abigail Iris?" Genevieve says.

Then I hear my sister walking up the stairs. When I hear her turning the doorknob, I say good-bye and hang up quickly. I hurry over to my bed on the other side of the room, where I pretend to be completely absorbed in taking off my shoes and socks.

"I thought you said you had homework," my sister says, looking over at my empty desk.

"You are not the boss of me," I say, walking over to my desk. I open my backpack and get out my spelling list and, despite how excited I now truly am, begin working in my best cursive on my homework sentences.

Chapter 4

My mom and I are sitting side by side on my bed, talking, and Victoria is still at her desk trying or pretending to read. I'm not sure which.

These are the details my mom found out when she talked to Genevieve's mom on the phone.

Genevieve's dad is going to drive up the coast, probably taking the long route so we can see the ocean. Yes, *we*—my mom and dad said YES!

There's a DVD player in their car, which is an SUV, what my dad calls a gas hog, but what my mom calls "a very safe vehicle for such a trip." Since Genevieve and I are the kids, we'll be sitting in the backseat, watching G-rated movies of our choosing the whole way there.

At this point, Victoria turns away from her homework and says, "How am I supposed to study in here?"

"You're right, Vic," my mom says. "I'm sorry, honey. You want us to go downstairs?"

"I'll go," my sister says, shaking her head, sighing, and picking up her notebook like it's the heaviest thing she ever lifted. She squints her eyes into a mean look, but I'm so happy about my trip with Genevieve that I just smile at her.

"What else?" I ask my mom when I hear Victoria stomping down the stairs. "Tell me the rest. I want to know everything."

So she continues.

"Genevieve's parents made reservations for six nights at the Sir Francis Drake Hotel. The two of you will have your own room."

"This is obviously so exciting," I say. "We can have room service."

"You'll be right on the cable car line," she says.

"I've always wanted to ride a cable car—my whole life I've wanted to ride one," I say.

"The hotel is also near the financial district, which is good because Genevieve's dad might have a little bit of lawyer work to do while he's away."

"He's going to work on vacation?" I interrupt.

"I suppose it's possible," she says, shrugging.

"What else? What else?"

"You'll be visiting Fisherman's Wharf and Chinatown and the Golden Gate Bridge."

"What about Lombard Street?" I ask.

"Oh yes," she says. "I'm sure."

I know about Lombard Street because Mrs. Aaronson is from Oakland, which I guess is near San Francisco, and she has a postcard up on the chalkboard of Lombard Street, and it's obviously the most crooked street in America and maybe even the world.

"I really want to see Lombard Street," I say. "And room service. I really want that."

My mom tells me that it's colder in San Francisco and more likely to rain than it is here, so I need to bring a raincoat.

I am so excited that I scream with joy after each and every detail, except the one about Genevieve's dad having to work while we're away.

My mom stands up and walks over to my closet like she's going to open it and then changes her mind. "Let's go get you a raincoat," she says, excited, turning around to look at me. She glances at the open book on my desk and asks me if I have any homework left. I tell her that I'm finished, even though I have one more sentence to write, but who can write a sentence when she has a raincoat to buy?

On the way to the mall in the car, my mom reminds me that I'm only eight and that I might miss the family on a week-long trip, and that it's okay if I want to change my mind at any point. The rest of us, she says, will be camping east of San Diego while I'm away in San Francisco. The rest of us, she says, will think about me and miss me. "But you'll be in a fancy hotel, Abigail Iris," she says, "having room service!"

I look out the window and remember last year's camping trip and how much fun it was. I remember Eddie and Cameron and Victoria and I sat on a blanket by the fire telling ghost stories and eating hotdogs and marshmallows until midnight after the grown-ups went to bed. I remember Eddie pointing out the Big Dipper, the Milky Way, and Ursa Major, which I couldn't quite make out but pretended to see anyway because I wanted to make him happy. I remember him putting his arm around me when it got cold and telling me I wasn't so bad for a girl and a sister. And then Victoria said, "What about me?" And then Cameron burped and the four of us ate burned marshmallows until our stomachs ached. We fell asleep that night under all those stars, even the ones I couldn't see.

Then I remember the mosquito bites on my legs and how much they itched and I remember that by the third day of our trip the soda was warm and Eddie farted on my arm to make Cameron and Victoria laugh, which they did.

I also remember the fight Cameron and Victoria had in the car on the way home about where to stop for dinner. I remember how cramped the car felt with all of us kids stuffed in the back two rows of the van with our tents and cookstoves and rolled up sleeping bags piled up all around us. And how cranky Cameron and even crankier Victoria couldn't get away from each other in the middle row because we were already on the freeway and my dad didn't want to stop. I remember we drove all the way home like that, skipping the dinner they were fighting about, and having to eat stupid cheese sandwiches instead. I remember staring at the back of Cameron's and Victoria's heads, which were turned away from each other the entire rest of the way back.

I think about how much a DVD player and a funny movie would have improved *that* drive home.

"What are you thinking about, Abigail Iris?" my mom says.

And I say, "Yippee! I'm going to San Francisco!"

ॐ

We go to Macy's because we have a credit card with their name on it.

"I can always wear last year's coat," I tell her, remembering our budget, although I obviously don't want to wear that old thing.

"No way, kiddo," she says, smiling.

We hold hands on the escalator and when I go to step off, she says, "Careful, careful, Abigail Iris," never for a second looking away from my two feet until they're planted firmly next to hers.

I drop her hand and run over to the girls' section, where I see the prettiest raincoat in the world. It has a white background and little pink flowers on it, and I want it so badly I nearly faint. I take it off the hanger, quick, quick, without even looking at the size, and miracle of miracles, it fits perfectly. I twirl around and around for my mom, who's laughing at what she calls my enthusiasm. I say, "Please, oh please. I love it. I'll be the best girl," I say.

"You already *are* the best girl," she says.

My mom always looks at the price tag before saying yes, but this time she doesn't. "You look adorable," she says. "Now, take it off so I can buy it."

I convince her to let me wear it up to the counter, and then I convince the nice woman who's taking my mom's credit card to give me the coat right back after she scans in the price and takes off the tags. My mom helps me put it on and the woman smiles at us both and waves 'bye.

Before we leave the mall, we stop by See's Candy to buy chocolate caramels for my brothers, sister, and my dad. My mom buys Victoria an extra piece, probably because she feels bad about sharing the details of my trip in the bedroom when my sister was trying to study. I ask for an extra piece too, but she says, "We bought you enough tonight, didn't we?"

And I must agree.

ॐ

"What's a vision?" I ask her on the way home.

"A vision?" she says. "Use it in a sentence."

When she says "sentence" I get a stab of guilt because I lied about being finished with my homework, but then I look down at my pretty new coat and touch the little pink flowers with my fingertip and get over it.

"Use it in a sentence," she says again.

"Billy Doil called me a vision today at school."

"Oh, Abigail Iris," she says, looking like she's tearing up for some reason, maybe because I'm going on a big trip and she's going to miss me or maybe because my coat cost a lot—I really hope it's because she's going to miss me.

"Is being a vision a bad thing?" I say.

"You're a lovely little girl, Abigail Iris. You're my lovely girl," she says.

Chapter 5

For the rest of the week, I am so distracted by thinking about my new raincoat and my vacation with my Only friend, I nearly fail third grade. On Friday before spring break, I forget my times tables and stare at my pop quiz. But I recover at the last minute and make myself concentrate on the numbers right in front of me.

At lunch I work hard not to brag to Rebecca and Cynthia about my upcoming trip with Genevieve. It's Pizza Friday so we all bought lunch, even though a person would have to be crazy to think that the gummy cafeteria pizza is the same thing as the kind a person gets delivered at home.

"Who wants my pepperoni?" Cynthia asks, making a neat little round pile on the side of her plate.

"I'll take it," Rebecca says before anyone else has a chance, and she lays out those round pieces on top of her slice wherever there's an empty space.

"On vacation, my family does not eat pizza," Genevieve says. "We try new things, like Brazilian food."

"I'm thinking about becoming a vegetarian," Cynthia says.

"Or Ethiopian," Genevieve says. "Or French."

Cynthia's going on vacation to a dude ranch in Texas, and her dad has her scared into worrying about eating nothing but rare steak. Cynthia has been one of my Only friends since kindergarten, and I know for a fact that she would make a terrible vegetarian. When she sleeps over my house, my dad makes us bacon and waffles and

Cynthia always says "yes, thank you" when he offers her extra pieces of bacon for being a sleepover celebrity.

Rebecca is going to math camp the way she does every spring break because Onlies parents like to encourage division skills. She even gets to leave school twenty minutes early today like she has a doctor's appointment so her dad doesn't hit too much traffic.

"I'm going to send you both a postcard," I say to Rebecca and Cynthia, "from the hotel." I am thrilled with the way the word "hotel" sounds, but after it comes out of my mouth, I worry I'm too braggy.

After lunch we all hold hands and walk in a slow circle around the playground together. I feel sad and happy all at once, like an important tooth I've always had is loose. "You are my only best friends," I say to Rebecca and Cynthia and Genevieve, and then we all hurry and line up for our classes when the bell rings.

Somehow Genevieve winds up way ahead of me in line the way she always does. I'm in the back, and Billy Doil runs up in line behind me, all out of breath from four square. "Easy quiz this morning, huh?" he says to me as we're walking into our classroom.

"Yeah, easy," I lie, so I don't lose my reputation as a multiplication whiz, even though I was so distracted by my recent good luck that there wasn't anything easy about the quiz to me.

"I hope you have a happy spring break, Abigail Iris," Billy Doil says.

"I will, Billy Doil," I say, and this time I'm not lying. And then I remember my manners. "You, too," I say. "I wish you a happy spring break, too."

༄

On Saturday morning at seven thirty a.m. I am ready to go. My mother has lent me her best suitcase, the one with wheels that she took on her honeymoon with my dad before Victoria or I were even an idea in her head yet. It's packed with everything Genevieve listed out for me.

1. Five pairs of underpants
2. Three pairs of jeans
3. Five pullover shirts
4. Toothbrush in sealed baggy
5. Hairbrush
6. One very heavy sweater
7. Victoria's hot pink nail polish, which I was surprised she let me borrow for the trip

8. Pajamas

9. Two going-out-to-dinner-in dresses

In addition, I have packed two things I don't plan to show anyone, even Genevieve:

1. My special sleeping-with rabbit

2. My very tiny flashlight

I plan to use the flashlight only in case I have an important emergency like I absolutely have to read in bed after everyone else is asleep.

"I will miss you, Old Man Cheeto," I say to my dad, who is drinking his coffee on the front porch while he waits for me to leave.

My dad rubs me on the top of my head, which he usually says feels like a lucky head, but this time he doesn't say anything. Instead, he squints off in the distance like he already sees Genevieve's car out there.

This is the most number of nights I have ever been away from home, and my parents both look way overserious this morning, like they're thinking about changing their minds or crying. Although I hate to see them sad, I hope it's crying they're thinking about doing.

I am wearing my raincoat even though my mother told me at breakfast that rain is not in the forecast anywhere in California today. Secretly, I'm glad it's not going to rain because my raincoat is new and beautiful with its little pink flowers, and I'm not ready for it to get all wet and soggy. *This raincoat is the next best thing to Heelys*, I am thinking, and I twirl around a little to show it off one more time to my dad in case he's forgotten I'm wearing it.

My mom comes out and tells me to be my

usual good and polite self and to listen to Genevieve's mom and dad as if they were my own. "And remember, honey, Dad will have his cell phone with us at the campground, so you can call if you need to."

When Genevieve's father pulls up, my mom and dad quickly take turns hugging and kissing me and pushing my ears into the sides of my head so they can look straight into my eyes and tell me how much they love me and how much they're going to miss me and how much fun they hope I have without them.

My sister and half brothers are still asleep, so I can't hug them good-bye. Instead, I hug my mom and dad an extra time each. Then, while my dad is putting my suitcase into the back of Genevieve's dad's car with him, and they are discussing the route, I open the door and sit down in the bucket seat behind Genevieve's mother, next to Genevieve.

Genevieve has on headphones and is already watching a movie that's playing on the

DVD player. My seat is big and comfortable, but instead of leaning back into it right away, I lean forward and look out my tinted window and wave good-bye to my mom and dad, who are busy waving back to me.

I roll down my automatic window so I can see better and I shout good-bye, and then when we've pulled away, I roll up the window again and sink deep into my seat. I let only one good-bye tear drop out of each eye before I wipe my eyes dry.

"I am so glad, Abigail Iris, that you made your case," Genevieve says to me while she stares at the movie. "This trip would be so boring without you."

Genevieve's mother is wearing a large straw hat, and she hasn't turned around to say hello to me yet. I look for her face in the mirror up front and see that she's wearing big, dark sunglasses. I remember that, like Genevieve, she is not a morning person.

"You are a vision," I say to Genevieve's

mother, and I hear her laugh a little. "Thank you very much for including me in your travel plans."

A cell phone rings and Genevieve's father puts in an earphone and talks while he drives.

"You are very welcome, Abigail Iris," Genevieve's mother says to me, still staring straight ahead.

"Oh, I almost forgot," Genevieve says, reaching into the pocket of the seat in front of her. She takes out a set of headphones and hands them to me.

"Plug yourself in," Genevieve says to me when I just stare at the headphones. I look up at the DVD player and see a place to plug in my headphones on the other side of Genevieve's.

And then my Only friend and I are off, on my first real vacation.

Chapter 6

We've been on the road for over an hour and the headphones sit in my lap because I am not someone who can miss any little bit of the movie and then enjoy figuring out what happened before I arrived. I'm a person who believes every second of the story counts and would rather wait and see the whole thing another time than miss one of those seconds. I told Genevieve this in my nicest, politest voice, but she had only lifted one of the headphones off one ear, so she probably didn't fully hear me. Or maybe she was too busy staring at the little screen in front of her to understand. All I know is she shrugged and kept watching.

Genevieve's mom tells me it's just fine to call her Shelly. "And call me Christopher," her dad says, waving into the rearview mirror.

"Do let us know if there's anything you need, Abigail Iris. We want you to be comfortable," Shelly says.

"Thank you," I say.

"Did you have breakfast?" she asks, turning around and lifting up her sunglasses without taking them off, looking at me with her big eyes.

"Yes, thank you," I say.

"We always stop on the way. By the time

we reach Gorman, we're always ready to get a bite to eat and stretch our legs," she says.

"Oh," I say, thinking that we've barely been driving and my legs are stretched just fine in this big car thank you very much.

"Will you eat something with us?" She lets go of the glasses then, and they fall back onto her nose.

"Okay, maybe just a little, thank you," I say.

"You don't have to say thank you after every word," she says, smiling at me. "We're very happy to have you with us. I know Genevieve is over-joyed that you're here." She turns to Genevieve, who is still very engrossed in the movie I didn't want to watch, and gives her a mother/daughter look that I recognize. It's a look my mom gives me when I've done something very wrong or haven't been as nice to someone as she wants me to be.

"Thank—," I begin and then stop myself.

Shelly adjusts her hat and then turns back around. "What a sweet little girl," she says to Christopher, and for the briefest second I don't know who she's talking about. But then I realize she's talking about me.

Genevieve laughs at something in the movie, but I don't know what's so funny, so I don't laugh with her. I know from past experience that watching a movie by yourself isn't nearly as fun as watching a movie with your best friend, and I think about that while I look out the window. I am also thinking that Christopher is a very good driver and that my mother would be pleased with the way he's winding us safely over these mountains. My ears are plugged, but they don't really hurt and I can still hear okay.

Shelly's pointing out the window. "There's the water tower. Get off here, hon," she says to Christopher, who's changing lanes and moving onto the off ramp.

I don't know what a water tower is, but I know there's something big and round on the mountain in front of us with the word GORMAN painted on it in blue letters. There's a store called the Antique Mall to the

left of us and around the bend there's an
Econo Lodge. We're pulling into the parking
lot of a place called Brian's Diner when I say,
excited, "We stayed at an Econo Lodge once.
My mom, my dad, my half brothers, and
Victoria. Last year on the way to my grand-
parents' house in Phoenix, we stayed at one of

those." I'm pointing at the motel and realizing that I may be a little too excited.

Genevieve finally takes off her headphones, and I almost repeat my Econo Lodge story now that both of her ears are free but decide not to.

"Come on, girls, let's get something to eat," Christopher says, sounding happy. He turns off the engine then and unlocks all of our doors at once.

We step outside onto the gravel. The air is a cold surprise, and I'm happy to have my coat on. The car parked next to us is covered in a thick, gray dust and looks like it's been here a thousand years. Someone's taken a finger and written *Wash Me* on the window. Genevieve yawns, covering the big O of her mouth with her hand. "My ears just popped," she says. "How are yours?" she wants to know, and right then, mine pop too.

"Better now," I say.

"Is that your new coat?" she says, eyes big and very impressed, I can tell.

"Yes, it is," I say proudly, smoothing it out

with my hands. I look down at it myself and fall in love with the little pink flowers all over again.

"Very, very pretty," she says.

"A vision," Genevieve's mom says, smiling at me. "Do you know what I'm going to buy you both when we get to San Francisco? Satin slippers. Remember the ones I got you last time that you outgrew, Genevieve?"

"I guess," Genevieve says, which means she's not really listening.

But I'm listening. Satin slippers. I have never heard anything like this, and I am obviously impressed.

Genevieve's dad is doing a big man stretch, his elbows pointy at his sides, his hands clasped together. He's moving left to right, left to right, like my dad does before playing basketball with Eddie and Cameron.

Shelly reapplies her lipstick without a mirror, which I think is very impressive, and then she drops the lipstick into her purse and snaps the purse shut. She takes off her hat and tosses it into the front seat of the car before closing the door.

"I want pancakes. Do you want pancakes, Abigail Iris?" Genevieve says, taking my hand. She apparently wants to be nice now, and I, for one, am very happy about that.

"Obviously, yes," I say, taking her hand and swinging it as we walk.

ॐ

We sit in a red booth and read from big plastic-covered menus. There are colorful pictures of hamburgers and french fries and a club sandwich, pictures of what looks like an iced tea and a salad with croutons and reddish-pink Thousand Island dressing, which is, by the way, not what I prefer. It's only ten in the morning and suddenly I don't want pancakes at all, but a chocolate milkshake because the picture of it looks particularly delicious.

"Milkshakes! Milkshakes!" Genevieve says, like she's reading my mind, and I decide that she really is my one and only Only best friend, even if she's grumpy in the morning. "Can we, Mom? Can we?" she says.

And Genevieve's dad says, "It's your vacation, girls. Anything you want."

Her mom shakes her head, but she's smiling and doesn't say no, which are both very good signs.

I am thinking this is pretty great ordering chocolate milkshakes, which are, by the way, Old Man Cheeto's blender specialty. And later there will be room service, which will be the only thing greater. Just then, Genevieve's dad's cell phone goes off and it's loud, what my mom would call an intrusion. He fiddles around in his pocket, making it vibrate, and the four of us ignore the loud buzzing for what seems like a long time. Finally, he takes it out of his pocket and flips it open.

"Yes," he says.

"Okay," he says.

"I see," he says.

The three of us are quiet while Christopher talks very seriously into the phone. He

scratches his cheek. He grunts and nods his
head although certainly the person on the
other end can't see him.

When the waitress comes up and slides a

glass of water in front of each of us, Christopher scoots out of the booth and stands up. He motions to Shelly before leaving the table and walks outside with his phone call.

Shelly sighs and shakes her head, and Genevieve looks at me and then picks up her menu. She holds it in front of her face again, like she's studying it, like everything she needs to know is right there in front of her.

"I'm going to hold on to this menu, if that's okay," she says to the waitress.

"Fine by me," the waitress says, pulling a pad of paper and a pencil out of her apron pocket.

And Genevieve keeps looking at the menu and looking at the menu, even after her mom has already ordered their eggs and coffee, and our fries and milkshakes, even after the waitress has scribbled everything down on the little pad of paper, even after she's walked away from us in her spongy shoes.

Chapter 7

Driving over a bridge into San Francisco, we pass a pink station wagon decorated all over with fancy, high-heeled shoes and tiaras.

I decide at that very instant that this is exactly what I'm going to do to my car when I grow up.

"Well, would you look at that," Shelly says. "We are definitely heading into San Francisco now."

After we left Gorman, I watched a movie with Genevieve and then took a nap with my head against the window. I've been awake for the last couple of hours though, watching the scenery. Already this San is much more interesting than San Diego.

Genevieve is concentrating on her third movie of the day and has missed the car covered in shoes and tiaras. She has also missed many other amazing things, in my opinion, like the man wearing a skirt and playing bagpipes in Monterey and the lady in Santa Cruz stopping cars to stick flyers on their windshields. I am too busy keeping my eyes open and pointing out the window to watch a movie.

"Okay, girls," Christopher says. "Just a few more minutes. And then, let the games begin!"

We haven't stretched our legs out since Gorman, and mine are beginning to feel pretty irritable. I would have given my own parents an earful by now, but I am saving my complaints to Genevieve's parents for when I've truly had it. I give each of my legs a turn pointing out its toes, and then I pull them back up like I do in class when it rains and we can't get out for recess.

It's almost dark, and the streets we are driving down after we have gone over the bridge are so narrow that I edge closer to Genevieve in case my door happens to get swiped off by a bus pulling away from the curb beside us. So she doesn't think I'm trying to edge into her seat, I pretend to be suddenly interested in movie number three and trying to get a better angle on it.

I am wondering if this gas hog is really taking up only one lane. I definitely feel like we're overlapping and will soon be in a horrible head-on collision. But no one beeps at us, so I concentrate on remembering how excellent Christopher's driving skills were on the rest of the trip. I decide that he wouldn't put his Only daughter's life in danger even if he is taking a phone call just when the streets seem to be getting their absolute narrowest.

"Yes?" he says.

"Uh-huh," he says.

"That's right," he says.

"California time," he says.

Shelly sighs and edges closer to her door while I'm thinking, *No, no, get back to the middle of this car.* Unlike Christopher, she has turned off her cell phone. Each time his rings, she takes hers out of the glove compartment and makes a point of pushing the off button just to show him, and then she slams it back in there.

I am thinking that they fight in a much slyer way than I am familiar with.

When we pull up to the Sir Francis Drake Hotel, I see full-grown men standing out front wearing white pantyhose and puffy shorts that stop at their knees and soldier hats, and I'm thinking that this is nothing like the Econo Lodge. It is like a royal palace. That's definitely what it's like in the lobby, which is full of the royal colors red and gold, and I tell Genevieve just that while her parents are busy checking us in.

"And we are the royal princesses," Genevieve says, making a very lovely curtsy.

I am overjoyed that the headphones are finally off my Only friend's head and that we are out of that gas hog.

We take turns sitting in every fancy chair we can find, crossing our legs very nicely and drinking our fake cups of tea.

When it is time for one of the soldiers to take our luggage upstairs, Genevieve tries sitting on the cart, but Shelly shoos her off. Genevieve takes my hand and we skip behind the luggage. We all squeeze into the elevator, Genevieve and I giggling and saying "excuse me, ma'am," "excuse me, sir," in our best princess accents as we make room for ourselves.

We get off the elevator on the ninth floor and follow the cart with our luggage on it down the carpeted hallway. The soldier opens the door to our room, and I am staring at his little silk jacket with envy. Then I look down at my flowered raincoat and remember what a lucky girl I am.

I am wondering if the soldier himself might be related to the true Sir Francis Drake, whoever he is. I decide to save the questions about Sir Francis Drake for later in case there is a too-quiet moment the way there sometimes is when I am with one of my Only friends and her parents, and everyone is counting on me to step in and fill it up with something.

"After you," the soldier says, stepping back out of the way.

I look around to see which one of us is "you," but everyone else is already walking in ahead of me, Genevieve first in line, obviously, just like at school.

Now, this is what I call a vacation, I think. Instead of sleeping on the ground, I will have a big, very decorated bed with tiny pillows stacked up on top of the real ones.

While I have been busy being very impressed, Shelly has walked around the room and looked out the window, inspector-like.

"We're facing the alley," Shelly says, sounding disappointed.

"It's a very quiet room," the soldier says.

"With a view of trash cans," Shelly says.

Christopher's cell phone goes off, and this time he hits a button without even taking the phone out of his pocket to look at it first.

"Come on, girls," he says. "I'll take you down for ice cream while Shelly gets this straightened out."

We leave Shelly to talk to the soldier. Genevieve and I race down to the elevator so we can each be the one to hit the button first. I win because, even if I am slower when it comes to lining up, very few can beat me when it comes to actual running.

"If my mom had let me bring my Heelys," Genevieve says, pouting, "I would have won."

"Maybe so," I say. "But I won fair and square."

Genevieve's pout is growing, so I decide to let her push the button that says Lobby when we get inside the elevator, so the pouting business won't go on all night.

The restaurant is very dark and quiet and elegant, and the menus the waiter hands us are so tall and heavy I'm afraid I will drop mine, and it will knock over my water glass and embarrass us.

"Two very large, very special hot fudge

sundaes," Christopher says. "And one very dry martini."

"Extra cherries on mine," Genevieve says.

And then we all hand the waiter our menus and I can breathe again. When our sundaes arrive, I think for just one moment about Victoria and how this is big enough to share with her without even complaining about it, but then I dig right in, ignoring the extra cherries on Genevieve's.

When I am down almost to the very bottom, Shelly walks up to our table, dangling a key in front of Christopher's face.

"Leave it to the expert," she says. "Girls, we've been upgraded." Then she takes a sip of Christopher's drink.

"You always make your case, Mom," Genevieve says, and I hear her long spoon scrape against the inside of her sundae cup.

We follow Shelly out to the elevator and let her push the button herself.

Our new room is on floor twelve. I'm too tired and impressed to look out the window at our better view. This time we have what Shelly calls "a sweet." She opens a door on one side of the living room and says, "This is your room, girls. Christopher and I will be in the room right on the other side of the sweet if you need us. Sleep tight, lovies." And she blows us both kisses.

I'm so tired that all I want to do is get in bed and settle down for the night, but I smile at her big and try to look enthusiastic. I'm wondering if all the Onlies get to stay up so late on vacation that no one is even keeping track of the time anymore. I'm wondering if they all get to sleep in sweets and eat ice cream sundaes for dinner and get into bed without even brushing their teeth.

"Good night, girls," Christopher says, shutting our door almost closed.

While Genevieve's in the bathroom, I hang up my raincoat very carefully in our personal closet, and then I sneak my sleeping-with rabbit out of my suitcase and slip him into bed with me. I can feel myself falling asleep with the lights still on, and I'm thinking it's a pretty good deal being an Only, and I make a note to myself to keep track of every second of it.

Chapter 8

Room service is even better than I imagined it. Here's what happens. A very friendly soldier woman knocks on our door and says, "Good morning, young lady," when I answer it, and then she rolls the cart inside and sets things up. As I'm getting back into bed, she lifts the silver lid from the plate and presents—yes, that's right—*presents* my silver dollar pancakes and eggs to me, and I am feeling very much like a princess. Then, she does the same to Genevieve's breakfast, which is eggs and turkey bacon and potatoes with little pieces of red and green pepper in it.

"Is this to your liking?" the soldier woman

asks Genevieve, and I'm sorry to say that my Only best friend is not nearly as impressed with the whole thing as I am. In fact, if it weren't for me saying, "Please, please, please, Genevieve, please," and really making my case, we might not have had room service at all and instead sat in the downstairs restaurant for our breakfast once everyone was showered and ready. My Only friend barely nods at the nice woman, and it is me who says, "I love everything on this plate and on her plate too, and thank you very much for coming here."

At the door the soldier woman smiles at both of us and says, "Let me know if you need anything else," and I decide right then that I will always, always, even when I am old and used to such things, be impressed with having my breakfast brought to me and presented.

"Should we both get in my bed and eat?" Genevieve says.

"Yes!" I say, and I jump out of my bed and into hers, and we get under the covers with the trays of food between us.

Right then, Genevieve's dad knocks on our door. "Good morning, girls. Hey there, Morning Glory," he says, popping his head inside.

"'Morning, Daddy," she says.

"Good morning," I say.

"Did you sleep okay, Abigail Iris? How about you, Morning Glory?" And he steps into our room then. His hair sticks up all over the place, and he's got the same stubble on his chin that my dad has when he wakes up, the stubble that makes me squirm and giggle and back away. When Christopher leans down and kisses Genevieve's cheek, I suddenly miss my dad and his prickly face a lot.

"You need to shave at once, Daddy," Genevieve says.

"Oh, I do, do I?" Christopher says, rubbing his cheek. He's wearing a white robe made out of towel material. It says Sir Francis Drake in the corner, just above his heart, in red stitching and obviously we want a robe like that too.

"Where'd you get that, Daddy? We want one!" Genevieve says, waking up now and becoming herself.

Christopher goes to the closet then and pulls two robes from hangers. We almost jump out of bed and tip over our trays of food, but Christopher saves us from a mess when he says, "Careful, girls. Easy now. Watch it." So we step out of bed slowly and carefully and our food is just fine, thank you very much.

He hands each of us our very own robe, but the robes are clearly meant for bigger people. Still, we put them on, squealing with happiness. They are very long, especially the sleeves, so Christopher helps us roll them up.

"Guests first," he says, helping me with my right sleeve and then my left, and then he helps Genevieve, who has already rolled one sleeve up pretty successfully. As we are climbing back into bed, Christopher kisses Genevieve on the top of her head and says, "Your breakfast smells good."

"We're starving," Genevieve says.

"Yes, starving," I say.

"*So* starving," Genevieve says.

"You don't look *so* starving," Christopher says, smiling at us.

"Oh, but we are," I say.

Christopher messes up my hair then, and I decide he is a very nice dad, even if he picks up his cell phone on vacation. "Your mom's in the shower," he tells Genevieve. "She wants to get an early start."

"Can we drive down the crooked street today? Please, please, say yes," Genevieve says.

He pulls on his chin and looks at us, first Genevieve and then me.

"Please, please," I say.

"Anything you angels want," Christopher says, snatching a piece of Genevieve's bacon before he goes.

≫

After Christopher leaves, we finally get to eat. We let the shiny silverware fall from the white cloth napkins, and then we spread the napkins out on our laps. I take a sip of my orange juice and it is pulpy and delicious and sweet. "Why does your dad call you Morning Glory?" I ask Genevieve.

"Because I am not a morning person—and neither is my mom."

"Oh," I say.

"My mom says the morning is bright and brutal and that those are two very good reasons not to like it."

"Hmmm," I say.

"I'm an afternoon person," she says, taking a bite of her eggs.

"It's what you prefer," I say.

"What are you, Abigail Iris?"

I consider this a minute. I take a bite of my very delicious pancakes and think about this. "I'm a morning, afternoon, and night person," I say.

"Really?" she says.

"I like to be around for all of it," I tell her.

"You know what, Abigail Iris? You *are*," she says, nodding and agreeing. "You're a morning, afternoon, and night person," she says.

The butter is a hard little ball that has its own tiny cup. The maple syrup is the best I've ever tasted. The eggs aren't quite hot enough anymore, but they're scrambled just the way I like them. "Want a pancake?" I ask Genevieve, who is already sticking her fork in my stack before I get the words out, which makes us laugh.

"This is the best morning," I tell her. "This

is the best hotel and the best bed and the best robe and these are the best pancakes and you're my best friend," I say.

"You're my best friend too, Abigail Iris," she says, stuffing a whole little pancake in her very happy mouth.

Chapter 9

It's the first real day of my vacation with my Only friend, and our early start is turning, in my opinion, into a late one.

Genevieve finished eating and immediately went back to sleep. She hopped out of her bed and hopped into my bed and pulled up the covers and asked for five more minutes.

I watched the clock on the nightstand, its red numbers flipping, and when five minutes were up, I said, "Wake up, Morning Glory." And then Genevieve asked for five more. We are on our *third* five minutes and I am finishing every last bite of my delicious breakfast when I hear Christopher's cell phone go off.

I move my tray over and get out of bed to open up the velvet curtains wide and let in the day the way my mother does each morning in Victoria's and my room to wake us. But instead of getting up, Genevieve pulls her pillow over her head. I peek out the door into the living room and see Christopher sitting at the little antique hotel desk, typing away on his laptop.

I pull the pillow off Genevieve's head and whisper loudly into her ear, "Wake up again, Morning Glory!"

"Hmm?" Genevieve says. "You're such a morning person, Abigail Iris. Is everyone else ready?"

I tell her about the phone call and the computer and the fact that Shelly still has not come out of the bathroom. "Ugh," Genevieve says. "We're never going to get out of this place." Then she opens her eyes big at me. "I've got an idea," she says.

Genevieve gets out of bed and slides into her fuzzy slippers so fast her feet never have to touch the carpet without them.

I follow her through the living room. She puts a finger up to her lips and we tiptoe. I see her father's back and his elbows pointing out in his white robe and I can hear the clicking of his fingers on his keyboard. But he doesn't hear us, and we walk right out the door into the hallway of the hotel in our big white bathrobes.

"Let's explore," Genevieve says.

I'm thinking this is not the best idea, but I'm only the guest, so I don't tell Genevieve no right away.

"What kind of explore?" I ask.

"You go up and I'll go down and we'll report back," Genevieve says. Then she tells me that she's going to beat me to the elevator this time. And she does, but only because I'm still standing there, confused, when she takes off.

I finally get what she means, and I run barefoot down the hall after her, hiking up my robe so I don't trip. I can feel the patterns in the fancy carpet on the soles of my feet, so I don't feel as jealous about not having fuzzy slippers, too.

Genevieve pushes the down button, and I push the up one and we wait together for our elevators.

"Good-bye, Abigail Iris," she says when her Down elevator arrives.

"I will miss you forever, my Only friend," I tell Genevieve, and then I am left standing in the hallway alone.

The light for my elevator comes on so fast that I don't have time to do what I obviously think is right, which is to go right back to our room and tell Shelly and Christopher that we must all band together and find Genevieve immediately.

I am expecting to be alone in my elevator the way Genevieve was in hers, but instead, when the doors open up, I am facing the same soldier who took our suitcases yesterday. He's standing next to a rolling cart with one suitcase on it. On the other side of the rolling cart is a business-looking man, pushing at a button on his watch.

"Good morning, miss," the luggage soldier says to me, saluting.

I salute back a little, step into the elevator, and stand on my tiptoes to push the highest number I can find, twenty-one.

"Ah, the Starlight Room. Excellent destination," the soldier says.

When the elevator opens on floor eighteen, the soldier tells the business-looking man, "After you," and they both get off and leave me to go up the rest of the way alone.

On the twenty-first floor, the elevator doors open again, and I walk around the carpeted floors slowly this time, letting my feet take their time to appreciate the carpet now that I'm not racing Genevieve.

The Starlight Room is a big circle restaurant on the top floor, which is obviously not open for breakfast. I am the only one here. Everywhere there are windows, and I run around the whole place, taking in all the views.

When my heart is completely pounding from all that running, I hit the elevator button and get back on to report to Genevieve. I almost forget what button to push to get to our floor, but then I remember, number nine, and I push it three times in a row just to make sure I go there.

When the elevator doors open at the ninth floor, I expect to see Genevieve standing there waiting for me, but she's not back yet, so I make faces at myself in a big gold hallway mirror. When I get bored doing that, I plop myself into the velvet hallway chair, pull up my knees, and snuggle into that chair, regal-like, as if I do this kind of thing every day.

I can hear the elevators going up and down and passing right by our floor, but the doors don't open. When an elevator finally stops at our floor, I jump up so I can give Genevieve a big leaping hug, but instead of Genevieve, I almost jump at an old lady who's carrying a little dog in her arms. The dog barks at me loudly, and although I have never in my entire life been afraid of dogs before, this tiny barking dog scares me, and I start to get a little nervous about where my Only friend Genevieve is.

"Calm down, Pierre," the old lady says, smiling at the dog instead of me. "There, there." And then she walks right down the hallway to her room.

It's taking so long for Genevieve to get back here that I'm thinking that maybe she has gotten captured by kidnappers, and I will never see her ever again.

And then I think that getting kidnapped is what my mother would call an unlikely scenario, and what has probably happened is that Genevieve has already gone back to our sweet without me. This is nothing that I would ever do to a friend. If she has gone back without me, I will be overjoyed that she wasn't kidnapped, but she will definitely not be my number one Only friend anymore.

I walk down the hallway, counting the number of doors until I get to ours. While I'm counting, I'm trying to decide if I will knock on our door or test it to see if it's locked and, if it's not, walk right in and sneak back to our bedroom as if I've been there all along.

I decide on the sneaking back in part, but the door is locked and I have to knock. I knock softly at first and then, when I hear a hairdryer going inside, louder. A lady who is wearing the same robe I am and who I have never seen before in my whole entire life finally opens the door. "Yes?" she says. "Do you need something?"

I look into the room to see if Genevieve or Shelly or Christopher are hidden in there behind her somewhere, but instead of our little living room, I see two beds, and then I remember that *this is floor nine and we moved to floor twelve!*

"No, thank you very much," I say, and I take off out of there and push the up button many times in a row until an elevator finally comes for me.

When I get off on floor twelve, they are all standing there, waiting for me. They are still in their big white bathrobes, and Shelly has a towel wrapped around her wet hair. I am thinking that no one in this hotel seems to have gotten off to a very early start today expect for that old lady and her dog.

"Where in the world have you been?" Shelly asks.

I can see that she is doing her best not to yell at me.

I look at Genevieve, who is biting on her lip and studying her fluffy slippers.

"I got mixed up," I say.

"We're just glad you're okay," Christopher says. "Isn't that right, Shel?"

"Yes," Shelly says. But neither of them hug me the way my parents do when they're just glad I'm okay. "We are very relieved. Come on, girls."

And then they turn and walk down the hallway, Genevieve and me trailing behind them.

"I have awful news," Genevieve says. "The absolute worst."

"What? Tell me right this minute," I say, unable to imagine what could make this moment any worse and wanting to get it over with immediately.

"There is no pool at all in this hotel, Abigail Iris. No indoor pool. No outdoor pool. No pool at all!"

"That's terrible," I say. But secretly I am relieved because at that very instant I realize that I have not remembered to pack my bathing suit. If there were a pool, Genevieve would have probably made me go swimming in my underwear and a T-shirt, the way Victoria did once in Ocean Beach, lying to me about no one being able to tell the difference.

Although I try hard not to forget things, I have no choice but to admit that I am a very bad packer.

"I can't believe they did this to me," Genevieve says. "Who ever heard of a vacation without a swimming pool? I am so completely sorry, Abigail Iris."

"We still have room service and the crookedest street in the world," I tell Genevieve.

"Girls!" I hear, and I look down the hallway and see Shelly and her towel-wrapped head. "Get in here this instant!"

"Coming, Mother!" Genevieve yells.

This time I don't try to beat Genevieve. I walk as slowly as I can down the hallway so I am in the back of our two-person line when we walk into our sweet to find out exactly what kind of trouble we have gotten ourselves into.

Chapter 10

We're standing outside the royal lobby, waiting for the car, and Shelly is still lecturing us about *not disappearing* and *no running off* and *don't you dare do that again.*

She's wagging her long finger.

She's shaking her head.

I'm trying to look like I'm listening to every single word of this important lecture. But, really, I'm wondering what my family is doing without me in San Diego right now and if Eddie and Cameron set up the tent right or if it's sagging in the middle.

"Abigail's parents trust us to take care of her, to take care of you both," Shelly says.

"I'm sorry, Mother," my Only friend says softly.

"You were in a bathrobe, Genevieve," Shelly says.

"I was in one too," I say, but I'm sorry as soon as I say it. I am not making things better. Everyone obviously knows that I was not only involved but that I was the one who got lost and ended up on the ninth floor. Everyone knows by now that I was almost bitten by a mean dog and that I'm very sorry and will never, ever, never do it again.

"It's not your fault, honey," Shelly says to me.

"It's my fault as much as Genevieve's. Maybe more," I say, although this isn't entirely true because it was Genevieve's bad idea and I only went along with it. Still, it was me who forgot where we lived.

"We're not just responsible for you, but for Abigail Iris, too," Christopher says. "We can't just lose your friend," he says.

"We didn't lose her," Genevieve says. "She's right here."

"You know what I mean," he says.

"It's a lot of responsibility, taking a friend on a vacation," Shelly says.

"I'm sorry," I say.

"It's not *you*, honey. I told you that," she says.

But it feels like me, and I'm thinking that when my own mom and dad get mad at me it's bad enough, but when it's someone else's mom and dad, it's worse than bad enough.

"We're only thinking about your safety," Shelly says, looking at Genevieve.

"Listen to your mother," Christopher says, and then his phone goes off and Shelly gives him a look that makes him ignore it completely. It's vibrating in his shirt pocket and it sounds like it hurts.

"You must turn that darn thing off," Shelly says, and she says the words slowly, her teeth clenched, and I, for one, would do exactly as she says. "This is a vacation, and we're supposed to be having fun." And the look on her face is anything but fun.

Shelly is talking to him quietly now, and I can't make out what she's saying, but I really want to know.

"It's okay, Abigail Iris," Genevieve whispers in my ear. "It was my idea to explore," she says.

Christopher's phone has stopped buzzing and Shelly has stopped scowling when the young soldier man steps out of the gas hog and hands Christopher the keys. I am so very relieved when we are in the car and on our way.

"Let's just start over, okay?" Shelly says, trying to be nicer now. "Let's get this day going. Buckle up, girls." She turns around, and I am fumbling with my seat belt and can't get the one piece to fit inside the other, which is something that happens to me when I am flustered, as my mother calls it. Shelly unbuckles her own seat belt and leans over to help me.

Finally my seat belt locks into place, and Shelly turns around and buckles herself up, talking to us. "Look, sweethearts," she says, "let's all have a good time."

Genevieve's face is pasted to the window. I put my hand on my best friend's knee and give it a little squeeze hello.

"How would you girls like to go to Chinatown and have Chinese food? How about some egg rolls and chicken chow mein and sweet-and-sour pork?" Christopher says.

I pull on my seat belt and move as close to Genevieve as I can, trying to get a look at her face. I think I see the tiniest curve of a smile, but I am not 100 percent sure.

"That sounds great," Shelly says.

"Doesn't that sound great, girls?" Christopher says.

I'm nodding for the both of us.

"Remember those satiny slippers I bought you last time, Genevieve? The ones you outgrew?" Shelly says.

Genevieve turns from the window then, but I can't tell what she is feeling.

"We'll buy those today. A new pair for each of you, just like I promised," Shelly says. "Remember, honey?"

Obviously I want to shout out that I remember all about those satin slippers, but I am the guest, so I wait for Genevieve to speak up first.

"They would make lovely keepsakes for you girls. What do you say, sweetie?" Shelly says.

And with that, Genevieve does smile a little bit and says, "Yes!"

Chapter 11

I wonder how this street can be legal.

I am no longer flustered, but I still double-check my seat belt many times as we go down the hill.

"Hold on, ladies!" Christopher says each time we make a turn.

Although we are in one of many cars following each other very slowly, Genevieve and I scream together like we're on Goliath at Magic Mountain. We put our arms up high in the air, and I feel my fingers touch the roof of the car.

"You're right, Gen," Shelly says. "This was a good thing to do before lunch." Then she

reaches in her purse and takes
out her lipstick as we go down
Lombard Street. I will be very
impressed if it's not smeared all
across her entire face.

We are all working hard to
pretend that this morning
never happened, even the
tiny fit that Genevieve
very recently had when
Christopher said we'd
drive down the

crookedest street in the universe only after the shiny new slippers and lunch.

When we get to the bottom of the hill, I feel like we should get off the ride and get right back in line to get on it again, and I have to remind myself that we're in the gas hog, not at an amusement park.

"Well, that was something," Christopher says.

"Let's do it again!" Genevieve says, and secretly in my head I am shouting right along with her.

"Maybe later," Shelly says. "First, I'm ready for some lunch."

"Shoes and then lunch," Genevieve says. "You promised."

"That was before we decided to do Lombard first," Shelly says.

Genevieve doesn't argue, but she doesn't look happy, either. She huffs and puffs, then puts on her headphones and stares at a movie that we already watched on the way up. Even though I am enjoying my leg and elbow room, I wish for an instant that Eddie was in the car to tickle Genevieve and tell her to loosen the heck up.

I look out the window and try to concentrate on remembering the pretty houses and flowers and the way everything looks, even though I can't see as clearly as I usually do because my mind is busy picturing those shiny shoes.

"There's the arch," Shelly says.

Driving into Chinatown under the gold and red and every-color-in-the-world arch is like driving into a movie, I am thinking. Maybe it's like that moment in *The Wizard of Oz* when everything goes from black and white to color.

We drive around and around Chinatown because it's hard to find a parking space, and when we do find one, it's not big enough for the gas hog.

While we're circling, I look in the windows of all the little stores, trying to spot my new keepsake shoes. Lots of stores just seem to sell things like CD players or gold-colored card tables or dolls with straight black hair, and I'm hoping that the shoes are not all sold out or that they didn't stop making them.

"Just spring for the parking lot, why don't you," Shelly says.

"I've never had to do that," Christopher says. He touches his shirt pocket, and I can see the outline of his cell phone in there.

We have all agreed upon a few things this morning. One, Genevieve and I won't disappear again without first telling a grown-up where we're going. And, number two, since he was so distracted by work he didn't even notice two little girls walk right past him and leave the hotel room this morning, Christopher will turn off his computer and cell phone and just occasionally check messages.

Shelly sighs and opens up the glove compartment and gets out her big, round sunglasses again. I catch a peek at her face in the mirror, and I am very impressed with her lipstick job. It doesn't look at all like she put on her lipstick while we were going down the crookedest street in the universe. She is a true makeup pro.

We finally find a space big enough to fit in and we all hurry right out. The air smells like my grandma's brisket, and although I can't wait to get my new silk shoes, I'm glad Shelly wants to eat first.

Genevieve grabs my hand, and we skip down the sidewalk together behind Christopher and Shelly, who are, I am very pleased to see, holding hands. My raincoat swings out around me as I skip, and I try to be careful not to swing it into anyone, especially the grown-ups who are busy hurrying down the crowded sidewalk. There has been no rain yet, but I am prepared.

"I am so glad you made your case and your mom let you come on this vacation with us," Genevieve says, squeezing my hand.

"Me, too," I say, "my Only friend."

It takes us as long to find a restaurant that Shelly and Christopher can agree on as it did

to park the car. I am now so hungry that even seeing two pigs hanging upside down in the window of the restaurant we are walking into doesn't make me lose my appetite.

"See," Shelly says to Christopher. "Now this place looks authentic."

This place looks crowded, is what I'm thinking. The downstairs is full of people talking in Chinese and bent over big bowls of soup. The waiter signals for us to follow him upstairs to a different room. Once we get up there, I notice Shelly frowning, but Christopher is already sitting down, looking at the menu.

I am pleased to see that there are plenty of pictures on the menu, and I point out the fried dumplings. "Those look like the same ones my dad orders for us from Hot Wok," I say.

"Try something new. Live a little, Abigail," Christopher says. "Venture out."

My feelings are hurt because I was only saying that they looked like the same dumplings, not that I wanted them. Even if I did.

When the waiter comes to our table, Christopher says, "Bring us your specialties. Surprise us."

As a rule, I like surprises, but I remember the pigs hanging by their feet in the window, and I'm a little worried about this one. I look over at Genevieve to see if she's worried, too. She's got her hair twisted up in the back with one hand, and with the other hand, she is trying to stick her chopsticks into it to make a bun.

"Let me try this on you, Abigail Iris," she says.

I turn my chair so my back is facing her, and I let her lift my hair up and twist it around in a circle. She pokes the chopsticks into my head, and I say, "Ouch!" louder than I mean to say it.

"That's enough, girls," Shelly says. "We're in a restaurant." And then our soup arrives.

There are lots of pieces of things that might be meat or might be vegetables floating around in my soup, and I wish I could have just ordered the wonton soup. I try to venture out and eat some anyway, but I'm thinking this is not nearly as good as room service.

"Not bad," Christopher says. "Huh, Shelly?"

Shelly gives him a quick little smile, and I'm thinking that maybe she wishes she ordered the wonton soup, too.

While we're waiting for the next course, Christopher announces that he's now going to check his phone messages. "And then I'm turning it right off again," he says to Shelly.

We are all very quiet and serious while he listens to his messages. I am watching his face to see what kind of news he is getting, and I don't like what I'm seeing.

"Darn," he says when he's through listening. "I've got to make a few calls."

When Christopher goes downstairs to make his calls outside, Shelly takes the things out of her soup that she doesn't like and dumps them in his soup bowl with her big spoon. When I catch her at this, she smiles her real smile at me, and I smile big right back at her.

"It's all an adventure, girls," Shelly says.

"Don't forget the silk shoes. Right after lunch," Genevieve says. "You promised."

"Absolutely," Shelly says, and then all at once the rest of our food arrives and our table is covered with steaming plates and bowls and so many smells that I decide to dig right in and try them all.

Chapter 12

The first thing I notice when we get back to the hotel room is that the beds are perfectly made and the whole room smells like lemons. Soft white towels have appeared and are hanging in the bathroom. They've obviously been folded by an expert. A strip of paper has reappeared over the toilet seat. The little soaps and shampoo bottles we used this morning are gone and in their place are brand-new ones. It was a mess and now it's clean. There's something magical about the whole thing, and it reminds me very much of the tooth fairy leaving a dollar under my pillow. *I wish I could invite these soldiers home with me,* is what I'm thinking.

The second thing I notice is that my satiny slippers are almost as beautiful as a pair of Heelys. Actually, they're more beautiful to look at, all red and shiny and bright, but that doesn't mean I can skate down the street in them. And sometimes a girl wants to skate down the street in her shoes—that's the way it is. Still, when I put the keepsake slippers on my feet, the satin is cool, and I feel like, not only a princess, but a ballerina.

We have purchased satin slippers, taken a cable car down a very big hill, and eaten chocolates that were wrapped up like tiny presents, and now Genevieve and I are doing our best ballerina moves, twirling and spinning around in our new slippers, when Shelly knocks on the door. Even though she's smiling, the rest of her face tells me that things are not as they should be.

"Look, girls," she says, "something has come up." She sits down on Genevieve's bed and pats the spots on both sides of her. "Come sit by me," she says.

I sit down, but Genevieve refuses to sit and

instead stands in front of her mom with a hand on her hip. "What now?" she says.

"Well, okay, don't get upset," Shelly says, as if feelings are a decision you make and not something that just happens.

Genevieve's already pouting before she hears the news.

"Your dad has a work emergency and we're going to have to head back early," Shelly says.

"How early?" Genevieve stomps her foot and her satiny slipper comes off and, despite the seriousness of all this, I almost laugh out loud.

"I'm sorry, girls," her mom says.

"What about the museum? What about our fancy dinner?" Genevieve whines, leaning down and putting her slipper back on.

"We're still going to have our fancy dinner," Shelly says. "We don't have to leave until the morning."

"Abigail Iris's parents aren't even home," Genevieve says.

"Christopher has already talked to your mom." Shelly looks at me. "Your brother's going to meet you at our house and drive you to the campsite."

"Okay," I say, trying to look disappointed out of loyalty to Genevieve, but feeling excited to see my family.

Sometimes you get bad news but it's really kind of good news in disguise, is what I'm thinking.

"I know this is a disappointment, girls, and we're going to make it up to you. Your father and I are going to make it up to you," she says, looking at Genevieve.

"How?" Genevieve says.

"I don't know yet, but we will. I promise," she says.

⁓

The fancy restaurant is almost dark, but there are red candles on every table, little flames making the people sitting at the tables glow. We're being led to our own table now by a very fancy man. He's wearing a black suit and the shiniest black shoes I've ever seen in my

⁓ 116 ⁓

entire life—even in the dark room I can see them gleaming. He calls Christopher "sir" and Shelly "ma'am." He calls us "young ladies." There is a woman playing the piano in a corner. She looks fancy too in a strapless dress, her hair curly around her face. There are purple flowers all around the room, and you can smell them. You can smell the steaks, which reminds me of Old Man Cheeto at the grill in his *World's Best Dad* apron, holding his very long fork and poking at whatever is sizzling in front of him.

"Don't you love orchids?" Shelly says to me. She is wearing a blue silky dress that swishes when she walks and her hair is up in a very stylish bun.

"I love them now," I say, because until this moment I wasn't exactly sure what they looked like.

"You're a gem, Abigail Iris," she says, laughing.

"A gem?" I say.

"You're something precious," she explains.

First I'm a *vision* and now I'm a *gem*—I'd

really like to know what's with these people lately.

Christopher is wearing a dark suit with a pink tie that Genevieve and I picked out. It is obviously very stylish and the perfect choice. He looks down at the tie now and adjusts the knot.

I have never been anywhere as beautiful as this, is what I'm thinking. *I bet they're going to present my food to me like that nice soldier woman did this morning,* is my next thought.

Genevieve and I are both wearing red dresses, but mine has a sash, which makes it, in my opinion, very unique. Shelly wouldn't let us wear our satiny slippers because she said they were *inside* shoes, which is okay because I'm wearing my favorite white sandals instead.

The fancy man pulls out my chair and I hop up a bit to sit down in what feels like a velvet throne. I'm half expecting him to call me "your majesty," but he doesn't. "There you go, young lady," he says, pushing my throne toward the table. "How are you tonight?" he

wants to know. "I am very good, thank you,"
I say. "And how are you?"

"Fine, fine," he says, smiling and nodding
while he hands me a menu.

"We're starving," Genevieve says to him. "Just starving."

"Yes, we are," I say.

"That's why you're here," the man says. "We can fix that."

I watch what Shelly does and try to do the same. She shakes out her napkin and puts it in her lap. I shake out mine and put it in my lap too. She makes sure the button on her dress is buttoned and I make sure that my sash is tied. Shelly takes a sip of her water and I pick up my glass and lift it to my own mouth. She touches her hair, making sure the bun's okay, and I touch mine. She sighs and I sigh too. Shelly looks down at her plate and silverware for a second, and I glance down as well.

"What in the world are you doing, Abigail Iris?" Genevieve says.

"Nothing," I say, lying.

When Genevieve's face disappears behind her menu, I look down again, noticing that my silverware is so shiny, so incredibly shiny that I can almost see my smiling face in the spoon.

Chapter 13

We have decided not to take the scenic route home.

Obviously, we are anxious to get back quickly so Christopher can get his important work done. And, besides, we have already seen everything there is to see on the way up.

"So are we all on board with the plan?" Christopher says over breakfast.

Instead of saying yes, I nod my head because my mouth is full of French toast.

We have not ordered breakfast in bed. We are eating in the hotel restaurant, which is very nice but not, in my opinion, nearly as nice as eating in bed. We have gotten an early start, even if some of us are looking pretty grumpy at the breakfast table.

Shelly is not hungry yet and has ordered only black coffee. When she's not drinking it, she's rubbing the sides of her head with her pointer fingers. Genevieve is picking at her eggs and staring at my French toast.

That's what you get for ordering off the adult menu, I think. I may be a morning, afternoon, and night person, but I am not feeling very generous.

"Did you remember to tip the maid?" Shelly asks.

"Got it," Christopher says. "Check."

Shelly frowns like he said he forgot instead of remembered. She seems disappointed that he keeps getting all of her questions right.

During breakfast, she has already asked three other questions:

Did you remember to pack the shampoo?

Did you remember my book?

Did you remember to check under Genevieve and Abigail's beds?

Check.

Check.

Check.

Because it is Christopher's fault we have to leave early, he is in charge of mostly everything.

Genevieve and I were in charge of packing our own suitcases though, so when Shelly looks at us, we both nod our heads before she can even ask.

"I know you two think you've packed everything," she says, "but think about it a minute and make sure. Let's be absolutely sure so that we don't have to turn around once we're on the road. Did you pack your pretty raincoat, Abigail Iris?"

"Check," I say, and Christopher smiles at me.

"At least we had a couple of nice days here," Shelly says. "It didn't rain once."

This is true and a secret disappointment to me. My mom had promised that the raindrops would hit my coat and then bounce off—and I really wanted to see that bouncing happen.

"Well," Shelly says. "I think in some ways it will be good to get back early. I'm still on vacation, after all, Genevieve. How often do we get time at home alone together?"

I smile supportively, although I think this sounds pretty boring.

"I don't like the eggs," Genevieve says, pushing her plate forward. "Can I get French toast instead?"

"It's too late for that," Christopher says. "No mind changing allowed this morning!"

Christopher signs the check that has been left on our table under four chocolates that are actually chocolate mixed up with mint. I was fooled by these very same candies yesterday after my room service breakfast, so I don't get tempted this time into thinking they're the right kind of chocolate, which is obviously the plain kind wrapped up like a present that we had after our cable car ride. I take mine and pass it to Genevieve, who actually likes these things.

"That was very nice of you, Abigail Iris,"

Shelly says. "Genevieve, wasn't that nice of Abigail to give you her chocolate?"

"Very nice, Abigail Iris," Genevieve says, and for a minute I think she's going to stick her tongue out at me real quickly, the way my sister used to sometimes when our mom wasn't looking.

Even if she does like my good manners, Shelly is still Genevieve's mother, not mine, and I think it's silly for Genevieve to be jealous.

"Who needs to go to the ladies' room before we get on the road?" Christopher says.

"Come on, girls," Shelly says.

The ladies' room is silver and gold and shining. I spend a few minutes looking at myself in the mirror after I have washed my hands to see how I have changed now that I have stayed in a fancy hotel with room service and eaten at a restaurant where I sat in a velvet chair.

Shelly stands next to me to apply her lipstick while Genevieve slides across the bathroom floor in her satin slippers. We are allowed to wear them since we'll just be in the car most of the day, but I tucked mine away at the bottom of my suitcase with my sleeping-with bunny for safekeeping.

"You're one of a kind, Abigail Iris," Shelly says to me, catching my eye in the mirror, and then she smacks her lips together to blend in her lipstick.

While Christopher and Shelly are making their best case about how much they should have to pay to the royal check-out lady in the lobby, Genevieve and I do not sit in each and every chair pretending to be princesses. Genevieve just sits in the first chair she sees and looks right in front of her like she's already watching her movie. I, for one, do not feel like sitting before I have to, so I walk around, saying my quiet good-byes to the whole place.

Next to a pile of maps, I spot a small pile of postcards of our royal hotel on a big desk with a sign on it that says Concierge. "Help yourself, sweetie," the royal man behind the desk says, and I say thank you and take three without asking if that's okay, one for Rebecca, one for Cynthia, and one for a keepsake for myself.

Everyone is suddenly very busy putting the suitcases onto a cart, and I obviously have no time to write and mail those cards now, so I quickly unzip my suitcase so I don't hold things up and put them in under my raincoat.

⌘

We stop on the way home only for take-out food and to find bathrooms, and I decide to watch every movie Genevieve puts in the DVD player. When we finally make it to Genevieve's block, I have watched so much television and sat still for so long that I feel blurry and wobbly, like I just climbed off a boat instead of out of the gas hog.

Christopher presses a button in his car somewhere and their garage door opens and lets us in. Our garage is way too full of stuff to ever park in. Where a car might be we have piles of boxes and bicycles and garage sale furniture that each summer my dad says he plans to refinish.

"Who's ready to get out?" Christopher says as the door closes behind us, and, of course, not one of us answers because everyone knows this is not really a question.

"We get to play until your brother gets here!" Genevieve says, suddenly lively, and she grabs my arm and pulls me out of her side of the car.

I race Genevieve through the kitchen and living room, up the stairs to her very own

bedroom, where we tag her door at the exact same instant.

"I'm sorry we had to come back so soon," Genevieve says to me. "Would you like to try on my Heelys to make up for it?"

I know for a fact that my feet are one full size smaller than Genevieve's, but obviously I say yes.

While her parents take everything out of the car, I skate around my Only friend's bedroom in Genevieve's Heelys, using her arm to keep my balance as I get adjusted to the feeling. My feet slip out a little in the back, but I don't care.

"You are the Only friend for me," I say to Genevieve.

❧

When I hear the doorbell ring, Genevieve and I are playing Go Fish, and I am winning, but I throw down my cards and race down the stairs.

I am so happy to see him, I jump into Eddie's arms from the fourth-from-the-bottom stair as if he were my dad, Old Man Cheeto himself, not my half brother Eddie. And because he isn't ready for me, I knock him to the ground.

"I have so much to tell you," I say to Eddie. I grab onto one of his hands with both of mine and help pull him up. "Do you want to see my satin slippers that came all the way from China right now or can you wait until we get to San Diego to see them?"

"Whoa," Eddie says. "Take it easy."

"Eddie," I say, "you are a true vision, and I am ready to go."

And then I remember my manners. "Thank you very much for a wonderful vacation," I say to my hosts, who are all gathered around us now.

" 'Bye, Abigail Iris," Genevieve says, and she turns and walks very slowly upstairs like she might cry if she has to stay there any longer and watch me get ready to leave.

"Thank you very much for keeping Genevieve such good company," Christopher says, and he puts out his hand, and we shake.

I save my special last good-bye for Shelly. I stand on my tiptoes and give her a big hug and kiss, the kind I only give out to very special people.

And then Eddie picks up my suitcase and we are out of there.

Chapter 14

Eddie's driving his $950 camp-counselor-money car, and I can't stop talking. I'm talking and talking and talking. I'm so excited about all that I am telling him that I can barely breathe.

"Calm down, Abigail," he says, all mumbling since he's doing that disgusting cleaning-under-his-nails-with-his-bottom-teeth thing now. I'm so energetic to report on all that I have done with Genevieve and Shelly and Christopher that I don't even care. I just keep talking.

I tell him about room service, about Chinatown, about the crookedest street in the world. I tell him about the Golden Gate

Bridge, the fancy restaurant, the white napkins, the orchids, and Shelly's pretty dress. I tell him Shelly can put her lipstick on without a mirror because she's obviously memorized her lips. I tell him that she can even put her lipstick on *without a mirror* while traveling down the crookedest street in the world!

"Now *that* I'd like to see," he says.

I tell him that when I grow up, lipstick will be part of my everyday life and that I'll have to memorize my own lips too. I tell him about Christopher calling Genevieve "Morning Glory" and about his constantly ringing cell phone. "He's a very important worker," I say.

"I bet," he says. "That house was something else. It's huge."

"When you're an Only, your house is sometimes bigger and your car always, always has automatic windows," I say.

"Is that so?"

"Yes, Eddie, that's so."

"What else?"

"Lots of leg room—even in the backseat."

"What, you don't have enough room back there?" he says, turning his head to get a look.

"I have enough room," I say, and kick my legs out to prove it. "But in an Only's car, you get extra. You get extra everything. When you're an Only, you have Heelys and sometimes you get pierced ears before you turn twelve. You have your own room and can paint it any color you want."

"Tell me more," he says.

"Well, room service isn't nearly as impressive when you're an Only."

"I'm sure," he says.

"Oh, and you get your own big bed at the hotel, and even when you lay in the middle of that bed and spread your arms out as far as they'll go, you'll never, ever reach the end of the mattress. It's impossible."

"That's a pretty big bed," he says. Then, "So you guys left early because Genevieve's dad had to work?"

"Like I said, Christopher is a very important worker."

Eddie nods.

"They can't seem to do without him," I say, which is what I overheard Shelly telling Genevieve last night when she tucked her in, right before she promised for the third time to make it up to her.

I tell Eddie about my slippers and the lanterns hanging from streetlights in Chinatown. I tell him how the pretty Chinese woman held

the slipper out to me and how I slipped my foot inside. "That's why they call them slippers," I say.

"I guess so," Eddie says.

And then before I can stop myself, I tell him about forgetting what floor we lived on and getting lost.

"What?" he says, both hands on the wheel now, looking up and catching my eyes in the rearview mirror, and for the first time his eyes aren't smiling.

"It's okay," I say. "I just went to the ninth floor instead of the twelfth floor."

"What were you doing on *any* floor alone?" he says.

"Oh gosh," I say.

"Where were Genevieve's parents?" he wants to know.

"In the hotel room," I admit.

"What were they doing in the hotel room? Why weren't you all together?"

"It was Genevieve's idea," I say nervously, "but I went along with it."

He shakes his head.

"Don't tell, Eddie," I say. "Please don't tell. I didn't tell on you when you stayed home from school that one time and you said you were sick, but then dad left for work and you didn't seem so sick."

"I *was* sick," he insists.

"You ate three bowls of cereal before I left for school, remember?"

Eddie smiles—even from the backseat I can see half of his smile. "I can be sick *and* hungry, Abigail Iris. They're not mutually exclusive," he says.

"They're not *what?*" I say.

"Never mind," he says.

"Well, you didn't seem sick to me—and I didn't tell on *you.*"

"I'm not going to tell," he says. "Of course

I'm not going to tell. I'm just glad you're safe, Abigail Iris. And I'm glad that you'll be vacationing with us," he says in a funny voice.

And I match his funny voice when I say, "And where will we be vacationing?"

Eddie says, "Campgrounds," and we both laugh.

I tell Eddie that Genevieve is sometimes a moody girl but that she's still my best Only friend.

"She's got that big house—what's she got to be moody about?" Eddie says.

I look out the window and think about this.

"Isn't she the one with all the cool toys?"

I'm still looking out the window, thinking.

"Doesn't she have the driver?"

"Yes," I say. "Genevieve has all of those things."

"So what's her problem?" he wants to know.

"Eddie," I say, turning from the window, "even Onlies aren't happy every single minute."

"Do you wish you were an Only?" he asks.

I think about this.

I think and think and think about this, and then finally say, "I'm one of many—and *you're* one of my many. It's not *always* the best thing to be an Only. Sometimes it is, but not always." And as the words leave my mouth I realize how true they are.

"Is Genevieve lonely?" he says.

"Sometimes maybe," I say. And suddenly I wish that I'd followed her up the stairs and hugged her one more time.

Chapter 15

Eddie's car may not be as fancy as Genevieve's, but I have the whole backseat to myself, so my body has no choice but to stretch out and fall asleep as soon as Eddie finally stops asking me questions and turns on the radio.

"We're here, Abigail Iris," Eddie says to me way too soon. "You'd better wake up because I, for one, don't plan to carry you out of this car."

I pretend to keep sleeping to see if Eddie, for one, really will leave me here in the backseat. When he bends down to pick me up, I open up my eyes wide at him and smile. "I knew you wouldn't leave me," I say.

Eddie is carrying my suitcase in one hand

and I hold on to his other. This is the same campground we go to every spring break, and I know how far we have to walk to get to our tent, but it seems farther in the dark. And it feels good to hold on to Eddie's hand. I'm glad I'm not wearing my satin slippers because even in my sneakers, I can feel the pebbles on the ground. For once, I am even glad I don't have

Heelys because I don't know anyone expert enough at wearing them to skate in the woods.

"You slept through a ton of traffic. Everyone's probably asleep by now," Eddie says. "We should try to be quiet."

"Shh," I whisper.

"Shh," Eddie whispers back.

"Shh," I whisper louder.

"Shh," Eddie whispers even louder.

And then I have to giggle so much that I just can't help myself.

"Abigail?" I hear. "Is that you?"

All I see is a big light shining right in my face, but I know that voice is my dad's, so I shout, "Yes, yes. It is I, Abigail Iris, home at last!" and I finally let go of Eddie's hand and take a flying leap in the direction of the flashlight, knowing that my dad will catch me.

"Oh, we missed you, honey," my dad, Old Man Cheeto himself, says. "Things really weren't the same without you."

"Were things absolutely terrible without me?" I ask. "How did you survive?"

"Well," Eddie says. "Someone seems to have a very good impression of herself. I'm going to bed." And then he rubs the top of my head, so I know he still likes me, and he takes my suitcase into our tent.

We may not have a camper like some of the families do at our campground, but we have the biggest tent I have ever seen. Walking into it is almost like walking into a regular house if the regular house was in the old days when everyone slept in the same room and went to the same school together.

Inside our tent, it is dark, and I hear Eddie pulling up his covers and the breathing sounds the rest of my family makes when they're asleep. But I know that they all will sleep even better when they know I have made it back safely. "I have arrived!" I say.

"Some people are trying to sleep," Victoria says.

"Sweetie," my mother says. "I'm so glad. Come here and give me one of your famous hugs."

I find my mother's airbed in the corner and crawl under the covers and hug her big. "I have satin slippers," I say. "My very own pair."

"Satin slippers. My, my. In the morning, I want to hear everything," she says.

"You are a vision," I say to my mother, and

this is true. She is a vision even if I can't see her very well in the dark.

I hug her once more, and then I find my brother Cameron's airbed, and I sit on his legs and play the drums on his back until he finally wakes up and pushes me off him. "Come get your nightgown on," my dad says. He's got the flashlight pointed at my suitcase, which he's opened on my airbed, which is already set up for me, thank you very much. But I hear something outside that can only be one thing, so before my dad has a chance to object, I grab my raincoat, which luckily is at the top of the pile, folded neatly on top of everything else, because I have to go out to investigate. My postcards are right there next, and I move them carefully to the bottom of my suitcase. I will write them tomorrow to my two other Only best friends, and I will use my *keepsake* postcard as part of my demonstration when I present my trip to my family.

"Just a minute, Dad," I say. "I think I dropped something outside."

I walk out through our tent door, but I don't look on the ground because I didn't really drop anything. I look up at the sky instead, and even though it's too dark to see the rain coming down, I can feel it hitting my face.

And, more important, I can feel it hitting my new raincoat and bouncing off.

My dad comes out and puts his arm around me. "Just a shower," he says. "Don't worry, honey. This won't ruin our vacation."

Obviously, I am not worried.

I may not be an Only, but I, Abigail Iris, one of many, am having a very happy spring break.

I have had breakfast in bed, eaten in fancy restaurants, and, finally, it is raining, and I am wearing my new raincoat, which is doing its job extremely well.

The one and only **Abigail Iris** is back!

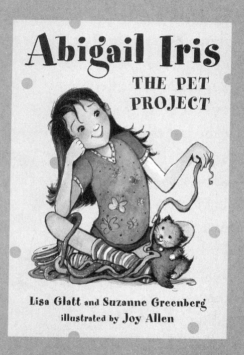

Read on for a sneak peek at Abigail's next adventure . . .

"He's about three months old, we think," the cat lady says to me. "Someone found him in the Albertson's parking lot behind the trash bin. Isn't he cute?"

I peek behind the teddy bear and see him, a black kitty. *Of course he's cute*, I'm thinking. *Is there anything cuter?* But I don't say a word because sometimes it's better to play it cool when you really want something, as my brother Eddie always tells me. He's a teenager, and although I don't prefer to admit it, he knows more things about the world than I do.

"It's my half birthday next week," I say to

the cat lady. "I'm thinking about getting a kitten this year."

"Is that right?" she says. The cat lady raises one eyebrow at me, which is something I wish I knew how to do with my face. My Only friend Cynthia knows how to wiggle her ears without touching them, and my brother Cameron can burp "My Country 'Tis of Thee" after he drinks a can of Sprite, but I don't have one single trick.

"Can I hold him?" I ask.

"Well, I don't know," she says, smiling. "You have to be very gentle."

"Of course," I say.

"He can be pretty wriggly," she says.

"I'm a good holder," I say.

She reaches in and picks up the kitten for me. I see a bright orange spot on his nose, and I think right away that this kitten must be named Spot even though it's a dog's name, and I hope he won't mind. She hands him to me, and I try my hardest to hold Spot gently without letting him wiggle out of my arms. He crawls up on my chest and buries his nose with the orange spot on it into my neck, and then he's very still, and I can feel his heart beating.

"I think he's scared," I say.

"He likes you," the cat lady says. "See, he's not even trying to get away."

My mother is handing a fat gray cat back to the cat lady and telling me it's time to go. "What a baby," she says about my kitten.

"Can we keep him, Mom, please, please, please?" I say, not being cool at all now. "A kitten is like half a cat and that would be the present I would most prefer in the whole world for my half birthday."

"He's very sweet," my mother says.

I'm waiting for her to say *but*, but I don't hear it right away, so I speak quickly before she can get it out. "He likes me," I say. "He's not even trying to get away. I would take care of him. I would feed him and change his litter box and buy him little toys with my allowance."

"Is that right?" my mother says.

The cat lady is giving her a business card

with her phone number on it. "You two need to think about this," she says. "A pet is a big responsibility. It's nothing to take lightly."

Whose side are you on, cat-rescue lady? I'm thinking, but my mother is putting the card in a special zippered compartment inside her purse, not just stuffing it into her pants pocket, so this went better than it might have.

"Maybe we'll bring up the idea to your dad tonight," she says to me as we pick up our bags and walk back toward the popcorn man and our car. "See what he thinks about a cat now that you all are older. Maybe it's time."

"You are the best, best mother," I say.

"Now, Abigail Iris, don't get your hopes up," she says.

"I won't," I say, but of course I do.

Lisa Glatt is the author of the Abigail Iris series, as well as *A Girl Becomes a Comma Like That* and *The Apple's Bruise*. She lives in California with her husband and their two cats. www.lisaglatt.com

Suzanne Greenberg is the author of the Abigail Iris series, as well as *Speed-Walk and Other Stories* and the coauthor of *Everyday Creative Writing*. She lives in California with her husband and their three children. www.suzannegreenberg.com

Joy Allen has illustrated more than thirty books, including the Abigail Iris series, *Princess Party*, and the popular American Girl: Hopscotch Hill School series. To research this book, she took a vacation to San Francisco with her grandchildren. She lives in California. www.joyallenillustration.com